Sam Discovers Soccer

Other books by Marion Renick

FIVE POINTS FOR HOCKEY

TAKE A LONG JUMP

FOOTBALL BOYS

WATCH THOSE RED WHEELS ROLL

THE BIG BASKETBALL PRIZE

BOY AT BAT

YOUNG MR. FOOTBALL

BATS AND GLOVES OF GLORY

PETE'S HOME RUN

NICKY'S FOOTBALL TEAM

THE DOOLEYS PLAY BALL

A TOUCHDOWN FOR DOC

Books by James and Marion Renick

STEADY: A BASEBALL STORY

TOMMY CARRIES THE BALL

Sam Discovers Soccer

by **MARION RENICK**
Illustrated by David Blossom

CHARLES SCRIBNER'S SONS · *New York*

Contents

1

Call the Emergency Squad

Sam poured milk on his corn flakes. He put down the pitcher and stretched.

"Mmmm. I like a lo-o-ong breakfast," he said. "I'm glad this is the first day of vacation. Aren't you, Mom?"

"My vacation won't begin until I make out the grade cards for my class," she said. "I must do that this morning."

"But you won't have to take me to Day Care anymore," Lori said. "Now Sam will always be home to play with me."

"I'll be at the playground most of the time," said Sam. "Playing baseball."

"Old batty baseball." Lori turned up her nose. "That's all you ever want to play."

"Yup." Sam yawned and stretched again. What he wanted most of all was to be on the Franklin playground ball team. If the team won the city playground championship, each player would get a City Champion patch. He had made up his mind to win one of those. He planned to go back to school next fall with one of those red-blue-and-yellow patches on his jacket.

"The playground doesn't open until tomorrow," his mother was saying. "Today you can keep Lori company while I work on grade cards."

"Okay." Sam reached for another piece of toast.

Lori had finished. She squirmed in her chair. "Are you going to eat breakfast all morning, Sam?"

"Why not? What's wrong with that?"

"Then we won't know when to start eating lunch," she said.

Mom laughed. "Lunch will be late today. I must take my grades to the school office first. Now, Sam, if you want to dawdle over your breakfast, you can wash your own dishes. I'm ready to do Lori's and mine."

Sam finished in two swallows. "I'm going over to Al's," he said as he hurried out the door.

He rode his bike to Alison's house on the next block. "I brought my ball and bat," he told her. "Let's start practice."

"What for?" she asked. "I'm not going out for the ball team this summer."

"But you said you were." Sam didn't understand her.

"I changed my mind," she said. "I found out that all the girls on last year's team are going to play again this summer. I won't stand a chance to make it."

"But I thought you wanted to win a champ patch," he said.

"I do! So I'm going in for crafts. If I make something in crafts class that is chosen for the City Playgrounds Handcraft Show, I'll win a champ patch, after all. Why don't you sign up for crafts?"

Before Sam could say he would rather play baseball, Alison's mother called to them. She wanted them to go to the store for her. They started out on their bikes.

"I'm glad yours has a basket, Sam," said Alison. "You can carry the bag of potatoes in it."

On their way back, they rode past Sam's house. Lori saw them and shouted, "Mommy is going to leave in a few minutes. She says for you to come home right away."

When Sam came, his mother was ready to leave for her school. "I'll be back in about an hour," she said as she drove away. "You kids stay close to home."

At once Lori said to her brother, "I'm not going to throw balls for you to bat. You always make me do that. Let's do something else."

"Let's ride our bikes," Sam said. "You can ride up and down in our drive. And I'll ride out in the street." He brought her three-wheeler and set it in front of her.

"I want to ride on your bike," she said. "In the basket."

"You're too heavy."

"I'm not any heavier than that sack of potatoes."

"The potatoes didn't wiggle. And you will," said Sam. "Something wiggly in the basket can upset a bike quicker than scat."

"Remember the lady who comes past here with the white dog in her bike basket?" Lori asked. "It wiggles. And she doesn't upset. I think you're as good a rider as she is."

Sam thought so himself. Lori kept coaxing. Finally he propped his bike against the step and boosted her into the basket.

"Sit in the middle and hold onto the sides," he told her. "Let your legs hang over the front."

He had a hard time pushing away from the steps. "Let's go!" Lori clapped her feet together. "Let's go!"

"Stop wiggling!" he yelled.

At last they got rolling. Down the drive and into the street.

"Whee-ee-ee!" Lori squealed.

Sam saw a pickup truck coming around the

corner. He made a quick turn toward the curb. Lori leaned too far to that side. They upset. She tried to jump out and knocked him over. Down he went, tangled in wheels and pedals, with her on top of him. She screamed. He just lay there. He didn't know how to get up.

He heard someone come running. A man's voice asked, "Are you hurt, kids?"

Lori kept screaming. Sam opened his eyes. The man was lifting Lori to the sidewalk. He came back and looked down at Sam. "Can you wiggle your toes?" he asked. Sam could.

"Can you move your head?"

Sam tried. His cheek was jammed against something hard. It felt like a pedal.

"We'll get this off you first." The man began carefully lifting the bike. "Then we'll see if you can stand up."

He helped Sam to his feet. Sam felt dizzy but he said, "I'm okay." He started to feel his cheek. His arm didn't move right. He looked down at it to see why.

"Uh-oh," the man said. "Looks like you broke it. We'd better call your mother. Do you live on this block?"

"Mommy isn't home," Lori sobbed. "And you're bleeding!" She pointed to the red spots spreading over Sam's shirt.

Sam bent his head to see. Blood dripped onto the street. He was scared to feel his face to find out where the blood came from.

Just then Alison rode up. "What happened? What happened?"

She stopped her bike with a screech of tires. "Sam! You're hurt!"

"Do you know this boy?" the man asked her.

"Sure. And that's his little sister. What happened? Did you run over him?"

"No. But my truck must have startled him when it came around the corner. He made too sharp a turn, to get out of the way. I think he should be taken to a doctor at once," the man said. "The little girl says their mother isn't home."

"I know," Alison said. "I'll go get my mom. She'll know what to do."

The man called after her, "Tell her to call the emergency squad. This boy is bleeding pretty bad."

"Ohhhh! Ohhhh! I want Mommy!" Lori kept crying.

Sam worried about his bike. The man tried to straighten it out, and also to quiet Lori. Alison came whizzing back.

"The emergency squad is out on a call. They told Mom they'll be here as soon as they can," she reported. "Here she comes now."

Sam felt a little better when Alison's mother took over. She gave a quick look at him, then told the man, "I'm Mrs. Finran, a friend of these children's mother. I tried to call her at school just now. They said she had left and gone to do some errands on her way home. I don't think it would be wise to wait for her. This boy—"

"Could you get in touch with his father?" the man asked.

"They are divorced. I don't know where his father is." Mrs. Finran hurried on. "This boy needs a doctor at once. Is that your truck over there? Who do you work for?"

"I'm in business for myself. Here, I'll give you one of my cards. I am—"

"Can you take Sam to the hospital emergency

room?" Mrs. Finran broke in, after a glance at the card. "I'll stay here with his sister. As soon as his mother comes, I'll send her to the hospital. Can you stay with Sam until she gets there?"

"I wouldn't think of leaving him alone." The man held out a hand to him. "Hang on to me, Sam. Can you walk to my truck? It isn't an ambulance with a siren. But it will get you to the hospital all right."

Sam was still dizzy. He remembered his mother always told him and Lori, "Don't ever get into a car with strangers." He wondered about this man. He looked back at Al's mother. She was nodding and saying, "It's all right. You'll be safe with him."

Dizzy as he was, Sam tried to make sense out of the big white letters on the neat red truck. GENERAL MAINT. Surely that wasn't the man's name. Or was it?

Then Sam noticed there was no place for a passenger to ride. As if the man knew what he was thinking, he said, "Don't worry. I carry a folding chair. Can you hold on to the door while I set it up for you?"

In two seconds the man was lifting him into the truck and saying, "Now, sit down easy. Rest your arm on your lap. Does it hurt?"

"Ouch!" Sam said as he moved it. He was quiet as they started, then he asked, "Do you know the way to the hospital?"

"Sure do. I know my way around inside the hospital too."

Sam wondered if the man was a doctor. But he knew a doctor wouldn't be driving a truck—even a small one like this—with GENERAL on it. Then he stopped wondering because his arm started to hurt worse.

In a few minutes the man said, "Here we are!" He pulled up behind an ambulance at a sign saying EMERGENCY ENTRANCE.

"Hey, General Maint, you can't park there!" A fellow in a rumpled white suit yelled at him.

"Oh, yes I can!" the general shouted. "I've got a kid here who has been in an accident. We can't waste time hunting for a parking place."

"Will you need a stretcher for him?" the man asked.

"No," said Sam's new friend. "Just hold the door open for us."

The hospital smell hit Sam as he wobbled inside. It gave him a cold, sick feeling in his stomach. His legs seemed to let go. He thought they weren't going to carry him down that long gray hall.

He heard calls for doctors on the intercom. He saw a line of people waiting on benches. Miserable as he felt, he noticed that not one of them was anywhere near as bloody as he was. This scared him even more.

The man with Sam took him to the head of the

line and spoke to the nurse in charge. "Hello, Mary. You can see how bad off this boy is. Get Dr. Kraft for us right away. We'll go into the emergency room and wait."

Sam thought it was like being on a TV show. Doctors and nurses buzzing around. Tall tanks on wheels. Cabinets full of frightening things. One doctor gave him something to swallow and a nurse gave him a drink of water. Then at last came a doctor with bright eyes behind shiny glasses. Sam's friend greeted him. "I'm mighty glad you're here, Dr. Kraft. This boy—"

The doctor was busy looking at Sam. "What happened to your face, sonny?"

"I fell off my bike," Sam mumbled. He didn't feel like talking. He wanted to go home. "Ouch! That hurts!" he cried when the doctor felt his arm.

"No wonder." The bright eyes smiled at him. "It's broken. We'll take x-rays before I set it."

Sam wasn't sure what they were doing to him. The general held his good arm and kept asking him questions. Did he like school? Was he glad about summer vacation? What was his favorite sport?

Sam said, "Baseball." He started to tell how he was going to make the team but stopped to listen to what the doctor was saying.

"Fractures of both the radius and ulna." Dr.

Kraft was carefully wrapping a gauze bandage over and under and around Sam's arm. Then white stuff was spread very thick over the bandage.

The general pointed to it and chuckled. "Plaster I understand. But not radius and ulna."

The doctor smiled. "Those are the two bones he has broken. To make sure they grow back together as they should, we have immobilized his forearm in this plaster cast which extends above his elbow and below his wrist."

The general asked, "Do you understand that, Sam?"

"I don't know." Sam was curious about the cast. He touched it with a finger tip. "It's getting hard," he said, surprised. "How long do I have to have it on?"

"All summer," said Dr. Kraft.

"Ohhh," Sam groaned. "There goes my patch."

"Nonsense. That patch will stay on your cheek until it needs to be changed."

Sam didn't even notice that he and the doctor weren't talking about the same kind of patch. He kept moaning, "All summer. Oh, no—not all summer!"

"Your face will heal long before that," the doctor said. "I'm talking about your arm. It will need to stay in the cast at least six to eight weeks. Maybe ten or twelve weeks. It will depend on how well your bones knit."

The door opened and Sam's mother looked in. "Is this where—" Then she saw him sitting on the high table. "Sammy! Are you all right?" She rushed to him and managed to kiss his good cheek in spite of the bandages. She squeezed his good hand and patted his head. "Oh, Sam, honey—do you hurt bad?"

"He has been a very brave soldier," the general said.

Sam was finished with being brave. His head hurt. His face hurt. His arm hurt. And he had just lost all hope of winning a champ patch. He leaned against her and sobbed. "Oh, Mommy! I can't play baseball all summer."

2

The Hero of Franklin Playground

The next morning Alison arrived before breakfast was over. "The playground opens at nine. I just heard it on TV," she announced. "We're going, aren't we?"

"Yes!" Lori shouted.

"Why should I go?" Sam boosted his heavy cast onto the table. "I can't play ball with this."

"I told you last night. You can go into handcrafts, like me," she said.

"Not with one hand."

"Well, come on anyway. You'll find something to do." She started to leave. "Let's go."

Sam felt so sorry for himself. "I can't go. I can't ride my bike."

"Oh, flapdoodle," said she. "We can walk. We always did before we had bikes."

"I'm ready to go," Lori said. She looked at her mother and added, "As soon as we brush our teeth. Do you want me to put the toothpaste on your brush for you, Sam?"

"Try to do it yourself, dear," Mom said to Sam. "The doctor wants you to use those fingers."

"Mommy, he'll squirt it all over everything," Lori said.

"I'll help you, Sam," said Alison.

"I'll help you into your jacket," said Mom. "You must wear it to keep your arm from getting chilled."

"I can do it myself," Sam muttered. He was already tired of having to be dressed and helped like a baby. And this would go on for *weeks.* He thought he couldn't stand it.

However, he changed his mind a little when he got to the playground. Everybody treated him like a hero. Even the teachers asked how he got hurt. Kids wanted to know how many stitches he had to have in his face. The lady who taught crafts asked, "Would you like us to make your cast look pretty?"

"Go ahead," said Sam.

The class got their paints ready. He took his arm out of the sling and rested it on the table. They first painted red flowers on the white cast. Then blue and yellow flowers. After that, they filled the empty spots with rainbow butterflies. "It's gorgeous!" the teacher said to Sam. "You'll feel cheered up just looking at it. Now, sit quietly for a few minutes till the paint dries."

Sam heard shouts from the ball field. "Strike three! You're out!" How he wished he could be the next batter up! All he could do now was run after balls that went out of bounds.

He hurried to do that as soon as the teacher helped put his arm back in the sling. Suddenly— oops! he almost fell. He discovered he could not run fast without both arms free. So he stood looking on.

Boys came to see why his arm was in a sling. They said, "Wow! Where did you get that neat cast?" Nobody asked how soon it would come off so he could play ball. The team had plenty of players.

He could see that some of them didn't play any better than he. If only he could keep up with them in practice, he could surely make the team. He began to count, "Summer vacation is for ten weeks. If my cast would come off in six weeks, there would still be a couple of weeks before the championship finals. Maybe I still have a chance!"

"Sa-a-am! Hel-l-lp me!" He heard Lori calling. He found her sitting on one of the swings. "I can't get started. Please, will you push me?"

When she was going good, he went back to

ball practice. As he passed the crafts table, he saw Alison cutting into a large plastic bottle.

"When I finish, and put a tail on it, this is going to be a rooster. See?" She held a feather at one end of the bottle. "I know something you can do with only one hand, Sam. You can poke around in that box of stuff over there and find some long feathers for my tail."

No matter how long a tail that bottle had, Sam didn't think it would look like a rooster. He went on to the ball field. For a long time he just stood there. Nobody treated him like a hero now. If he started after a fly ball, one of the other boys always beat him to it. Once he tried to get a long high one. Again, he was too slow. He was left way out beyond third base. He saw a bunch of boys there hollering and bumping each other and kicking a large ball.

All of a sudden the ball came straight at him, close to the ground. It was too big to catch with one hand. Without thinking, he spread his feet and stooped a little, so that he trapped it between his legs. He let it slide to the ground. Quickly he stepped back on one foot and gave the ball a hard push with the side of his other foot. It went rolling toward the boys.

He heard a shout. "Where have you been?" Sam looked around.

"I mean you!" A man wearing a playground supervisor's badge pointed at Sam and came closer. "Where have you been keeping yourself? A boy who handles the ball that way should be playing soccer with these kids here. Instead of breaking his arm." The man smiled and nodded toward Sam's cast.

"Soccer? Is that what they're playing?" Sam thought he knew all about that running and kicking. "We call it kickball at school."

"Kickball and soccer are as different as dog paddling and water skiing," the supervisor said.

"I myself think soccer is the most exciting team game in the world."

"I like baseball," said Sam.

"A player gets cheated in baseball,—uh—what's your name?" the man stopped to ask. When Sam told him, he went on. "Sam—think how long a ball player waits on the bench for his turn to bat. Soccer players are in the game every single minute. Any instant the ball can come to them, and they have to do something with it. Just as you trapped that ball a minute ago. Then got rid of it with a fast kick. That was a good play, Sam. You really ought to try soccer."

Sam wanted to say, "I like baseball." But the man was still talking.

"We are starting a city playground soccer league this summer. We need players. Now I think that kick of yours shows that you're a nat-ural-born soccer player. Of course, you can't play much this summer because of your arm. But you could hang around the field here and learn the game. Then *next summer* you will be sure to make my regular team. If our Franklin play-ground team wins the most league games, every boy on it will get a City Champ patch. You'd like that, wouldn't you?"

Sam nodded. He was thinking, "Next summer I can win a champ patch for *baseball*. Why should I play soccer?"

Still, the supervisor had said, "I think that kick of yours shows you are a natural-born soccer player." Nobody had ever told him he was a natural-born baseball player. In fact, the baseball coach once told him he had to learn to hit the ball before he could play at all.

He was thinking this over, when he heard, "Sa-a-am! I've been looking all over for you!" Here came Lori. "The big kids grabbed all the swings, Sam. I'm going to stay with you."

Sam thought his broken arm was enough trouble without having her too.

"Mommy told you to look after me," she reminded him.

Sam had an idea. "See that long table over there with kids sitting around it?"

"What are they doing? Eating?" She was interested at once.

"No, nutsy. They are painting pictures and making things. They're having lots of fun. Al is there. You go over with her. The teacher will give you something to make."

Lori wasn't sure she wanted to do that.

Sam saw the soccer players were working the ball toward his side of the field. He wanted to get rid of Lori quickly. He took the best way he could think of. He said, "You run along over to that table, and wait for me. If you don't bother me, I'll give you a present."

"What will it be?" she asked.

"I don't know," he said. That was the truth! "But it will be something you'll like. Now get going—or I won't give it to you."

"Oikey-doikey." She trotted off. "Don't forget my present."

He forgot at once, for here came the ball rolling over the grass. He drew back one foot and swung it forward just at the right moment. The crossed laces of his shoe smacked against the ball. It went a long way. "Hey, take it easy!" yelled the boy who chased after it. Another boy yelled, "Nice kick!"

Sam was pleased. Here was something he could do even with a broken arm. He hung around waiting for more chances to kick. He tried to see how many players were on a soccer team. They were going so fast he couldn't count them. All he found out was that the boys called their supervisor "Ricco" or "Coach."

After a while Ricco came to stand beside him. "See what I mean? This game has a lot more action than baseball," he said.

"I guess so," Sam answered. "But is it as much fun?"

Ricco smiled. "Come back tomorrow. We'll have the field marked off with white lines. Then you can see some real playing. We're lucky to be at a school on the edge of town, with all this

open space back of it. There's room for baseball
and soccer."

Here was the ball again—coming too fast for
Sam to kick it. He tried to stop it with his foot.
The ball hit his shoe and bounced off. A player
kicked it away. Sam wished he had made the
kick. But Ricco said, "That's the stuff, Sam.
Sometimes letting the ball bounce against your
shoe toward a teammate can be a smart play.
You'll be a good man for our team." Then he
hurried off, calling to some players, "Nix on that
pushing from behind! It's against the rules!"

Sam waited for another chance to kick the ball.
It didn't come his way. He went back to baseball
practice and stood around till his arm began to
hurt. So he went home.

Lori met him at the door. "Sa-a-am! What did
you bring me?"

3

Lori's Present

"Where's the present you promised me?" Lori asked again.

Sam thought fast. He said, "I told you to wait for me, and I would bring you something. You didn't wait. So you don't get it."

"I did wait. But you didn't come. You told me not to bother you. So I came home by myself. And you know Mommy said you should look after me. She won't like it when I tell her you let me come home by myself."

"Well, don't tell her," Sam said.

"I'm going to, because—" she poked her finger into his middle, "—you didn't keep your promise." She started to walk away.

"Stop! I'll give you a present, like I promised."

"When? When I go to the playground with you tomorrow?" she asked.

Sam had a bright idea. "I'll give it to you if you *don't* go. Do you promise to stay home?"

"Oikey-doikey. But don't forget my present."

Next morning Sam stopped at Al's house to walk to the playground with her. She asked, "Where's little Tag-along?"

Sam told her why Lori stayed home. Alison said, "If you don't know what to bring her, how about my rooster? I'm making it for my Mom. But if it doesn't turn out right, you can give it to Lori."

Sam was thinking of something else. He was wondering what he would do at the playground. Watching baseball practice was no fun when there with nothing for him to do. He decided to go to soccer practice. At least he might get the chance to kick the ball sometimes. He found a space like a football field already marked off. It had a white line across the middle with a circle in the center. The boundary line at each end of the field had two cross marks in the middle. Ricco was pointing them out to the boys. "The space between these two marks is the goal," he said. "You must kick the ball across it. That scores a point for our team."

"But there should be a post at each end of the goal, with a cross bar to join them. And a cage behind," said one of the players. "I played soccer last year in Cincinnati, and—"

"Those cages are only to catch the ball," Ricco cut in. "We can do without them—especially since we have our ball chaser with us." He waved at Sam.

A tall, red-haired boy said, "At our school, Ricco, we don't have goal posts that are stuck in the ground. We set up yellow plastic markers. They are as high as regular goal posts. Eight feet, I think. They are made so you can put a pole across the top for a cross bar. You have to kick the ball under that, and between the posts, to score a goal."

Ricco nodded. "I ordered two pairs of those for our field here."

Suddenly the boys started to laugh. Sam went closer to see what was so funny. The red-haired boy said to him, "Look at that crazy cat!" Then he laughed harder than ever.

Sam saw a small spotted cat rolling in a patch of weeds growing along the goal line. It leaped into the air, whirled around, then pounced on the weeds again. It took a long stretch from its pink nose to its stringy tail. It nipped the green leaves, sneezing and twitching its whiskers. It hugged itself, jumped straight up, and sneezed again.

Sam laughed so hard he had to hold his broken arm to keep it from shaking.

"I'll bet that's a patch of catnip," Ricco said. "Cats go wild over it."

"Shall we pull it out by the roots?" one boy asked.

"It would be easier to chase the cat away," said Ricco.

"I'll get rid of it," said the boy from Cincinnati. "I'll kick it in the slats."

"Oh, no, Bill!" The red-haired boy stopped him. "Let's find its owner."

"It doesn't seem to belong to anyone," Ricco said. "It was meowing around here all day yesterday. I suppose the smell of that catnip brings it."

"Here, kitty, kitty!" some of the boys called.

"That's right. Coax it away," Ricco said. "Then we'll cover the patch with something." He looked around but found nothing to use.

"Take my old jacket!" Sam tried to slide his good arm out of the sleeve.

"Thank you very much, Sam," Ricco said, helping him. "I don't think we'll hurt it any. We seldom get the ball this near the goal. Here, Red—take Sam's jacket and help him spread it over the catnip patch."

"Scat! Scat!" A spotted streak shot out of the weeds. Red plopped Sam's jacket down and patted it flat.

"Cover the whole clump, so the cat can't smell it," Ricco said. "Then he won't come back."

"In Cincinnati we never let a skinny old cat hold up soccer practice," Bill grumbled. "Let's get started."

"Save your breath to run with," Red told him. "We can't start till Ricco tells us what positions we'll play."

Already Ricco was pointing to different boys, saying, "You play left fullback. You play right fullback. . . . You three men will be our half-backs—left, right, and center halfback. And you five fellows will be the forward line—two on the right, inside and outside; two on the left, inside and outside; and *you*—from Cincinnati—at center forward.

"Now let me see—" he stopped and looked the boys over, "—that's ten players. We need one more. A goal keeper. A goalie has to guard twenty feet of goal line. He needs long arms and legs. Red, how would you like to play that position?"

"Fine—if I can play on the same team with Bill Bettridge."

Ricco laughed. "So you think you'll have an easier job with our player from Cincinnati on your side."

"I'm better at making goals than at defense,"

Bill said at once. "The fullbacks can help Red defend the goal."

Ricco lined up a second team. It took all the boys that were left. "I wish we had a couple more for substitutes," he said. "Sam, hurry up and get that cast off. We need you."

Sam was still standing near his jacket. Red came to take his place in front of that goal. Ricco laid the ball on the ground in the white circle in the center of the field. He backed off, blew his whistle, and the game started with each center forward trying to kick the ball toward the other team's goal.

The boys ran and scuffled to get the ball. Sam soon noticed that Bill Bettridge got to it first and kicked it oftener than anyone else. He noticed, too, how Red kicked the ball away every time it came near his goal. Sam decided that even with a broken arm he himself could play goalie. Goal keepers just stood there and kicked the ball away. Then a ball came in high, and Red reached up to catch it. He got rid of it at once by throwing it far out to a teammate.

"Are soccer players allowed to catch the ball?" Sam asked him.

"Only the goalies are," said Red.

So there was no place on a soccer team for Sam until his cast was off. And by that time he would be playing baseball, he thought. He moved around to the side of the field. Almost at once the ball came out of bounds there, a little above the ground. He gave it a smack with the front of his foot. He was pleased with his kick.

"What did you do that for?" Bettridge yelled at him.

Sam was puzzled. Yesterday Ricco praised him for doing the very same thing. Now the coach blew his whistle, picked up the ball, and came to explain.

"Sam, the boys were just horsing around yesterday. Today we are playing by the rules. The rule is that if a ball goes out during the game, a player steps outside the line and throws it back in. This player must be on the team which did *not* touch the ball last before it went out."

"So I get to throw it in." Bettridge reached for it.

"No, you don't!" boys shouted. "You kicked it last. Our side throws it in."

"Sure, I kicked it last." Bettridge laughed at them. "I kicked it so it would hit somebody on the other team and bounce out of bounds. That way I made you guys touch it last. So my side gets to throw it in. Right, Ricco?"

"That's right," Ricco agreed. "And it was a smart play too. But what do you boys say we set up some practice for Sam? We owe him a favor in return for the use of his jacket."

"Sure," one boy said. "It kept the cat away."

Bettridge quickly stepped out of bounds with the ball and threw it to a teammate. Next he got it and began to move it down the field with short, easy kicks.

"Is that hard to do?" Sam asked Ricco.

"Try it for yourself. The boys left an old soccer ball lying over there in the grass. Go get it and practice dribbling."

"Dribbling?" Sam asked. "That's basketball."

"It's soccer too. But in soccer you do it with your feet," Ricco said. "Go ahead and try it. For your own special practice."

At first Sam kicked the ball too hard. Ricco had warned him that would let the other team get it. So he tried walking beside the ball, moving it along with gentle shoves. After a while he began to wonder why he was doing this. Baseball was the sport for him. He decided to go over to the ball field. But he couldn't leave without his jacket. And if he took it away, the cat might come back. The boys wouldn't like that.

"Fooey with soccer!" he said. He kicked the old ball hard enough to send it almost to the baseball field. As he went to pick it up, he saw a runner make first base, then go on to second.

Somebody yelled, "Go for third! That's the way to win your champ patch!"

Sam gave his cast a hard slap. "Aw, heck! Why do I have to have *you!*"

He stayed there, just watching. When the twelve o'clock bell rang, he remembered the soccer ball. He gave it a couple of long kicks to carry it back. As Ricco picked it up, he asked Sam, "How did you get along with dribbling?"

"Well—uh—" Sam was still thinking baseball.

"Keep working at it. What you need is a ball of your own—to kick around the yard, up and down the street, anywhere you go. Get the feel of it in your feet. That's how you learn to make it do what you want it to." Ricco started toward the school with a ball under each arm. He turned back to add, "Don't forget your jacket. See you tomorrow, Sam."

Sam walked home with Alison. She said, "I couldn't make my rooster's tail stick on. I think I'll make a hippopotamus out of that bottle tomorrow. What did you do this morning?"

"Nothing."

"Then how did you get all that dirt on your jacket?"

"It played soccer." Sam laughed. He felt something against his leg. He looked down and there was the spotted cat from the playground. "Scat!" he said.

"Don't chase it away. It likes you," said Al. "Look how it is trying to climb your leg."

"I think it's after my jacket. This was covering a catnip patch," Sam said. "Ouch! It's digging its claws into me. Get it off!"

"It sure is ugly," Al said as she set the cat on the ground.

They both stamped their feet and shouted, "*Scat!*"

The cat stiffened its legs and glared at them. "Me-*ow-ow!*"

"Let's don't pay any attention to it," Sam said. But the cat stayed close to his ankles all the way home.

Al asked, "What about your jacket? You'd better not let your Mom see it looking like that."

When Sam got home he left his jacket beside the front steps. He was too hungry now to think what to do about it.

The minute he was inside the door, Lori came running. "Sa-a-am! What did you bring me?" She saw his empty hands and howled, "You broke your promise again! I stayed home all morning because you said you would bring me a present if I did. And if I didn't tell Mommy you left me alone yesterday. So now I'm going to tell her."

"No, don't." He grabbed her as she started for the kitchen. He had another of his bright ideas. "I did bring you something."

"I don't believe you." She gave him a look. "What is it?"

"Something you will like. Something—" he pushed open the screen door and looked out. Hurrah! The cat was still there, pawing and sniffing at his jacket. He scooped up the animal with his good hand and brought it to Lori. "There! It's for you," he said. He tried to put it in her arms. She wouldn't take it, so he set it on the floor.

"Is that what you brought me?" She turned up her nose. "It sure is funny-looking. All spotty brown and black and white."

"It's speckled," Sam said brightly. "Did you ever hear of a speckled cat before?"

"No-o-o." She stooped to look at it.

"Of course, you didn't. Speckled cats are very rare," he said. "Pat it and smooth its fur. You'll see how pretty it is."

She tried that. "It is soft as feathers," she said, surprised. "Hello, kitty. Look, Sam, it's licking my finger. Oo-oo-oo. Its tongue feels like a cheese grater. . . . Nice kitty—*oh!*"

The cat sprang to the back of a chair and walked along the top like a tightrope walker. Lori laughed and took it in her arms. "Mommy!" she called. "Look at the cute little cat Sam brought me!"

Lori came into the kitchen with it just as Mom opened the refrigerator door. *Zzzt!* The cat leaped in. Mom shrieked, "It's a cat! Get the broom!"

Sam looked in the refrigerator. The cat was balancing on a melon like a trained seal on a ball. Lori lifted it out. She smoothed its spotted fur. "You are a very cute cat," she said.

The doorbell rang. Sam went to answer it. He was surprised to see the chubby-faced man who was standing there. He still didn't know the man's name, so he called him the first thing that popped into his head.

"Hello, General Maint! Come on in! . . . Hey, Mom! It's the general. You know—he took me to the hospital in his truck!"

Lori had followed her brother with her cat in her arms. As the man stepped inside, it jumped onto his shoulder with a wild *"Mee-ow!"*

"What goes on there?" He turned his head, trying to see. He was holding a box with both hands, so he could not reach for the cat.

"It's my sister's cat. I'll get it off. Lean over a little," said Sam.

The man bowed his head. "Ouch!" The cat held on.

Sam lifted it off, all the while calling, "Mom! Come here!"

"Oh, dear." Mom groaned when she saw what had happened. "I hope the cat didn't hurt you, Mr. —"

The man broke in with a laugh. "Maybe it's trying to be friendly." He turned to Sam. "I just stopped by to see how you are coming along after the accident. When you get tired of looking at those pictures on your cast, here's something to do with your other arm." He held out his box.

"Thank you," Sam remembered to say. "What is it?"

Zzzt! The cat leaped at the box. The lid flew off. Five hundred jigsaw puzzle pieces came down like hailstones.

4

Sam in Trouble

The visitor laughed till his chubby cheeks squeezed his eyes shut. Sam howled at Lori, "Look what your cat did to my brand-new puzzle!"

"Oh, dear." Mom sighed and shook her head.

"No harm done," the man said. "This simply makes it more of a puzzle than ever."

"You are very kind to bring it to Sam," she said. "I'm glad you came, because I don't think I ever really thanked you for getting him to the hospital so quickly that day. By the time I got there, I was too upset to tell you how grateful I was, Mr.—Mr.—Why, I don't even know your name! Sam calls you General, but—"

"Maybe that's because I'm a plain, general-average person," the man said with a twinkle in his eyes.

"We think you are a very special person—kind

and helpful," Mom said. "I wish we could do something for you in return for your kindness to us."

Crash! The cat leaped to the top of a lamp and knocked it over.

"Oh, dear," Mom sighed again. "There goes the light bulb."

"I have some on my truck, Mrs. Blake," the man said. "I'll go get one." He was off at once.

Mom said to Sam, "Generals don't wear coveralls. Why did you start calling him a general?"

"That's what somebody at the hospital called him. It's the name on his truck. Look out the window." Sam pointed.

"All I can see is A-I-N-T. What does that mean?" Lori asked.

Mom laughed. "It means he *ain't* a general."

Sam laughed too. "You'll see the whole name when he swings the truck door shut," he said.

The man left the truck door open and came bounding across the lawn with a light bulb. But after he screwed it in the lamp did not light.

"Must have jarred a connection loose when it fell," said he. "Would you like me to take it along and fix it?"

"I would appreciate that very much." Mom smiled. "I'm not handy with tools."

"I could fix it if I didn't have this cast," Sam said. "I think."

The visitor was wrapping the cord around the lamp. "I'll have this back in a day or so. I want to keep a check on Sam here till his arm gets out of that fancy doghouse."

They all stood in the doorway to wave good-by to him. The cat started out with him. It stopped to sniff at Sam's jacket, which still lay by the steps. Sam tried to pick up his jacket before Mom saw the dirt on it. He was too late.

"What in the world happened to that?" she asked. "It looks as if you rolled in the weeds. But certainly you didn't—not with a broken arm!"

"No." Sam slowly shook his head. "I took it off and some boys played soccer with it."

"The washer will have to play with it next. I hope I can take out those stains." She reached for the jacket just as the cat jumped at it.

By the time they remembered to look at the name on the truck, it was out of sight.

"I don't care what his name is, I'm going to call him General anyway," Sam announced.

"Come on, kitty," Lori said. "I'm going to get you a saucer of milk." When she opened the refrigerator door—*zzzt!* in went the cat.

"We'll have to put a stop to that," said Mom. "We don't want it climbing over our food. Besides, it could freeze to death if it accidentally got shut inside."

"It heard me say milk, and it knew where the

milk is," Lori said proudly. "It is a very smart cat."

"It is also a nuisance," said Mom. "But if we're lucky, it won't stay with us long."

"I won't let you leave, kitty." Lori petted it. "I'll make you so happy that you will never want to go away."

The cat was still there two nights later when the general brought back the lamp.

"It's good as new," he said, unwrapping the newspapers around it. He set it on the table and started to fold up the paper. He began to chuckle. "So this is where the sports page went! Wait a minute till I see how my favorite team stands in the league."

"Sit down and be comfortable while you read," said Mom.

As soon as he held up the paper to read it, *crash!* The cat took a long leap, tore through the paper, and landed on his chest.

"By jingo! That cat is an acrobat." The general's merry face poked through the hole in the paper. Everybody laughed. He tickled the cat's ear and said, "You are indeed a fearless feline."

"Feline." Lori said the word, listening to the sound of it. "Feline. That's a nice name for kitty. Here, Feline. Come here, Feline."

"Feline is its last name," the general said. "All cats belong to the feline family."

"Call it Fearless," said Sam. "Fearless Feline.

Don't you think that's a good name for it, General?"

The general wadded his newspaper into a ball and tossed it at the cat. "Catch it, Fearless."

Fearless swung at it with both front paws, but missed. The wad landed at Sam's feet. Without thinking, he kicked it across the room. The general turned to the cat with a shake of his head. "You will never make the baseball team, Fearless. Better stick to acrobatics."

"Do you think I can make the ball team, when my arm is well?" Sam asked, full of hope.

The general answered in his slow, easy way. "You act more like a soccer player, I think."

"Baseball is my game." Sam began telling this kind, jolly man his dearest wish. "I want to make the playground team, so I can win a City Champ patch. I didn't make it last year. Now, I guess I'll have to wait till next summer. Maybe I'll make the team then."

"So you didn't get on the ball team last year." The general nodded slowly. "I see. Well—there's more than one way to skin a cat. With a kick like you just made—and with your left foot, too—maybe you should try soccer."

"I like baseball," Sam said.

"Okay," the general agreed. "But remember, Samson, sometimes a boy is smart to change his mind."

"Fearless changed his mind," Lori said. "At

first he wouldn't let me pet him. Now he purrs when I rub his stomach. Want to hear him?"

The general said he must hurry off. He left with a cheery, "See you all later!"

Sam remembered how Ricco, too, had said he should be a soccer player. But he wanted to play baseball. Next day he did not go near the soccer field. He hung around baseball practice. There was nothing for him to do. So many were out to make the team that every runaway ball had a regular comet's tail of boys streaming after it. He decided to go home and watch baseball on TV. "I'll learn from big league players," he promised himself. "Then I'll beat this whole bunch of guys to a place on the team next summer."

He stopped at the crafts table to ask Al if she was ready to leave. She said, "I want to finish my hippopotamus. Or maybe it will turn out to be a big pig."

Lori had stayed home to play with her cat. So Sam started home alone. He came to a crowd of people on the lawn of a very large old house. The doors stood wide open. All the furniture was outside on the lawn. Chairs and chests, beds and blankets, pots and pans. People were poking around in the boxes, pulling out things and saying to one another, "Look at *this!*" One man called to his friend, "I just found a box of old comic books! Should we buy them?"

Sam wished he could buy some. He looked for price marks, but found none. He had no money anyway. His allowance was always gone the day he got it. More people came to look at the comics. Sam was surprised to see one of them was Bill Bettridge. "Are you on your way home from soccer practice?" Sam asked.

The older boy stared at Sam as if he never saw him before. Sam said no more. He picked up a comic and got interested in it. Once, though, as he turned a page he glanced across the table. Bettridge was slipping a little stack of comics under his shirt.

Sam thought, "Why, that's stealing." He quickly looked away. He hoped Bettridge didn't notice. If the other boy knew he had been seen, he might do something to frighten Sam into keeping his mouth shut about it.

Then Sam decided Bettridge surely had a good reason for putting the comics under his shirt. He probably wanted to leave both hands free because he was going to pick out some more to buy.

Sam moved on, looking at tennis rackets with broken strings, a folding canoe, and an enormous curling horn of dirty brass. He wanted to blow the horn, so he looked around to see if anybody was looking. Most of the people were watching a red-faced man who stood on a chair shouting. He was holding up a large white pitcher. He kept yelling in a sing-song, "I'm a-bid-a-bid-a-bid-a-bid six-six-six dollar-dollar-dollar. Who'll bid-a-bid-a-bid fifty-fifty-fifty . . . I'm bid-a-bid-a-bid fifty . . . Who'll bid-a-bid-a-bid seven-seven-seven . . . Who'll bid-a-bid-a-bid-a-bid fifty-fifty-fifty . . . Do I see fifty-fifty-fifty—"

Suddenly Sam spotted Alison standing far back on the other side of the crowd. He raised his good arm high and called, "Hey, Al!"

She saw him and started to edge around the crowd to meet him.

The red-faced man went on with his bellow. "Fifty-fifty-fifty . . . Who'll make it eight-eight-eight . . . This is your last chance, folks. Here it goes. Seven-fifty once . . . Who'll give an eight? Eight-eight-eight . . . Seven-fifty twice . . . Seven-fifty . . . and SOLD—to the young gentleman with his arm in a cast."

Sam looked around. "Do you see him?" he asked Alison. He was interested in anyone who also had his arm in a cast.

Just then a stranger came up to him, saying, "Here's your pitcher." It was the one the red-faced man had been holding.

"It isn't mine," Sam said. All the same, the stranger put it in his good hand.

"You just bought it for—" the man looked at the paper on his clipboard, "—seven dollars and

fifty cents. If you will give me that amount—and the sales tax, too." He figured on his clipboard. "That comes to thirty cents. Making a total of—uh—seven dollars and eighty cents you owe us."

"How could I? I didn't buy this. I don't even have any money." Sam began to wonder if this was a trick Bettridge was playing on him. He said again, "I didn't buy anything."

"Of course you didn't," Al spoke up.

"You keep out of this," the man told her. Turning back to Sam, he snapped, "You can't crawfish out of your bid. Do you mean to tell me you didn't bid on this antique water pitcher?"

"Whatever it is, I'wouldn't even want it. Honestly!" Sam tried to give it back to him.

The man thumped his clipboard and looked very cross. "You made the highest bid on this article. And the law says the buyer must pay up."

"Let's get out of here!" Alison took off.

Sam started to follow. He forgot he was still holding the pitcher.

5

Sam's Secret Deal

"Stop!" the man with the clipboard yelled after Sam.

At the same time a thin little woman with a very large purse grabbed Sam. "You must be the one," she said. "They told me a boy with his arm in a cast had bid on it and got it. May I look at it?"

She took the pitcher out of his hand. She turned it upside down and looked at the bottom. She snapped her fingernail against it. "Perfect," she said. "Will you sell it to me? I'll give you two dollars more than you paid for it."

"He hasn't paid anything for it yet, missus." The man with the clipboard hurried up behind Sam. "He made the highest bid—"

"I never did!" said Sam.

"You raised your hand when the auctioneer was asking for seven-fifty. Nobody went any

45

higher. So you were the highest bidder. And you sure-as-shooting have to pay for it."

"I didn't raise my hand!" Then Sam remembered. "Oh—I was only waving to Al."

"Whatever you were doing, you did me a big favor." The little woman patted Sam's cast. "I must have this old pitcher for my kitchen shelf. I got here too late to bid on it myself. I would be so happy if you would sell it to me."

"Fork over seven-fifty plus tax, missus. And it's yours," said Mr. Clipboard.

She opened her big purse and paid him. "But I promised this boy two extra dollars," she said with a nod at Sam.

"That's between you and him, missus. It's my opinion he doesn't deserve it." The clipboard man walked away.

"I think you do." She smiled at Sam and tucked two dollar bills between the fingers sticking out of his cast. "If anyone else had been the highest bidder, he surely would have kept this sweet old pitcher for himself."

Sam hurried to the sidewalk. He looked for Al but could not find her. However, when he got home, Mom said, "What happened to you? Alison just called and I couldn't make out what she was talking about. She seemed to think you got yourself into some kind of trouble. What did you do?"

"I didn't do anything."

"You must have," Mom said. "She said something about the law."

"All I did—" Sam began to laugh, "—all I did was wave at her. And I made two dollars."

"What?" Mom asked. He was laughing so hard she couldn't understand what he was saying.

"I made two dollars. Look!" He laughed so hard he had to hold his cast steady.

"What are you going to buy with it?" Lori asked.

Mom wanted to hear the whole story. When he told it, she laughed too. Lori still wanted to know what he would spend his money on. "Candy would be nice," she suggested.

Sam knew exactly what he wanted. "One of those things that you step on a pedal and it flips up a baseball for you to bat," he said. "Where do they sell those, Mom?"

"At the sporting goods store, most likely."

"Do you think I could get one for two bucks?"

"If there's any money left over, you could buy candy," said Lori.

"Tomorrow we go to have Dr. Kraft look at your arm again," Mom said. "I think there is a sporting goods store near his office. You can stop in there and find out what your money will buy."

"When are we going to the doctor? Morning or afternoon?" Sam asked.

"Right after lunch."

"Good! I can hang around ball practice in the morning," Sam said. "I don't want them to forget about me. I want to be out there playing as soon as I get this off." He thumped his cast. "Do you suppose the doctor will take it off tomorrow?"

"No, dear." She smiled and shook her head.

"He said six to eight weeks, *if* it heals right. If it doesn't, you will have to start over, with a new cast."

"I sure hope it's healing right." Sam put his ear to the cast. "I don't hear it knitting. Didn't you say the bone is supposed to knit?"

"Yes—but you can't hear it, silly," she said. "Now, don't worry. Dr. Kraft will tell us tomorrow how your arm is doing."

"I wish he would say I can play baseball soon," said Sam.

Next afternoon he kept his fingers double crossed for good luck as he went in to see the doctor.

"Are you getting enough to eat, boy—having only one hand to feed yourself with?" the doctor greeted him.

Sam nodded. "I have trouble with pie, though. And Mom has to cut up my meat."

The doctor reached for Sam's broken arm. "Well, well," he said, "I see you can cross your fingers. Can you uncross them?"

Sam did. He felt foolish that the doctor had caught him with them still crossed. But Dr. Kraft said to Mom, "This shows he has a good reaction in that arm, Mrs. Blake. That's fine."

"Do you mean you will take the cast off?" Sam asked.

"What's your big hurry?" The doctor was feeling Sam's upper arm now. "I should think you would want to keep that handsome cast on until the flowers fade. Or do you want it off so you can eat pie faster?"

"No." Sam shook his head. "I want to play baseball at the playground this summer."

"That arm won't be ready to swing at a ball for a long time," the doctor said. "Don't they have checkers games at the playground?"

"He has made up his mind to play baseball," Mom said.

"Sometimes—" Dr. Kraft looked at Sam over his glasses,"—sometimes we'd be smart to change our mind."

Sam wished the doctor would change *his* mind, and take off the cast. Instead, Dr. Kraft said, "I want to see x-rays of Sam's arm, Mrs. Blake. Take him across the hall to the x-ray room."

Afterward, on their way down in the elevator, Mom asked Sam, "Have you changed your mind about playing baseball? You don't still want that gadget that throws balls, do you? How can you bat?"

"I'll bat with one hand," Sam said. "I need to practice keeping my eyes on the ball. The coach told me that last summer."

She left him in front of the sporting goods store. She said she would meet him later at the car.

He did not go inside the store at once. He looked in the window first. It was a wonderland. Red-white-and-blue tennis rackets and shoes. Big safety bubbles for the heads of motorcycle riders. Baseball bats in all shades from chocolate to vanilla. New baseballs white as marshmallows. Near them—at last!—he saw what he was looking for. A short tube of red plastic on a green plastic base with a pedal. The box it came in lay beside it. In the box were two balls. They looked like baseballs but he knew they were light as feathers. You were supposed to put one on top of the red tube, get set with your bat, then step on the pedal. The ball would pop into the air just high enough for you to swing at it. You didn't have to swing hard. Sam thought such easy swings would not hurt his arm. If he had that little machine, the other boys would not get too far ahead of him in baseball. He could hold batting practice all by himself.

He pressed his nose against the glass, trying to read the price marked on the box.

A voice said, "If you want inside, why don't you use the door instead of the window?"

Sam looked around. There stood Bill Bettridge. He was surprised that the soccer player stopped to speak to him. "Oh—I—uh—was trying to see how much that costs." Sam pointed.

"I can tell you," Bettridge said, as if he knew everything. "Four ninety-five."

"Oh." This was a blow to Sam. He didn't want the other boy to know how disappointed he was. So he said nothing more.

Bettridge asked, "Are you going to buy it?"

Sam shook his head.

"Why not?" Bettridge asked. "Don't you know what it's for? Or won't your mother let you buy it?"

Sam tried to laugh as if that neat gadget meant nothing to him. "When it's marked down to two dollars, maybe I'll buy it," he said. "And maybe I won't."

"Do you have two dollars on you?" Bettridge gave him a friendly look.

"Sort of." Sam didn't want to say Mom was keeping it for him.

"For two dollars," said Bettridge, "I know where you can get something that's worth a lot more than that plastic thing."

Sam was not interested. Bettridge said, "It's a bargain that a boy who likes soccer can't afford to miss."

"I like baseball," said Sam.

Bettridge went right on talking. "I noticed you

kick a soccer ball like you have played since nursery school. So how come you weren't at practice this morning? Ricco brought that old ball for you. But you didn't show up."

Sam didn't want to say he had gone to baseball practice. Now, he remembered the boys hadn't even noticed he was there. Yet here was the best player on the soccer team asking why Sam had missed soccer practice. Besides that, the soccer coach had brought a ball for him to work with. The baseball coach had only told him to stand back farther so he wouldn't be in the way.

Again, Bettridge didn't wait for Sam to speak. He was saying, "Even with your arm in a cast, you ought to work at kicking. You want to make the team next summer, don't you?"

The team Sam wanted to make was the baseball team. Yet none of those boys ever talked to him like this. Bettridge went on, "Really, that old dead ball isn't good enough for a kicker like you to practice with. You should have a new one. You need a ball with life and bounce to give you real practice." He stopped, looked around, and asked, "Did you say you have two dollars?"

Sam nodded. Bettridge patted his shoulder. "Then you're all set! For two bucks I can get you a brand-new soccer ball. Like I said, it's a bargain you can't pass up. Look at the price on that soccer ball in the window."

Sam looked. It was ten dollars and ninety-five cents.

Bettridge held out his hand. "Give me your money, and I'll bring you the ball tomorrow at the playground."

Sam still did not want to say his mother was keeping his money for him. Also, he wondered if he really wanted to spend it for a soccer ball. Yet he *did* like kicking one. And he couldn't buy the little batting machine anyway. So he said, "Show me the ball first."

Bettridge didn't want to. Finally he gave in. "Okay. Pay me at soccer practice tomorrow. I'll bring you the ball." He started to go, then turned back to add, "Don't tell anybody about this. Other kids might want the same deal if they heard about it. I can only do it for a good soccer player like you."

Sam felt as if he had been chosen for the Athletes' Hall of Fame.

Mom was waiting in the car for him. "Did you find the pitching gadget you want?" she asked.

Sam nodded. He had almost forgotten it.

She opened her pocketbook. "Do you want to go back and buy it? Here's your money."

"It costs too much," he said. "I can't buy it."

"I'm glad. I don't think you should try to bat, not even easy swings with your good arm." She started to shut her purse.

"I'll take my money, though." Sam held out his hand. "I want to buy something else." He told her the bargain he was getting.

"Why is that boy doing this for you?" she asked. "You aren't good friends, are you?"

"No-o-o." Sam answered slowly. "I guess he's crazy about soccer and wants everybody to play it."

"Just be sure it isn't your two dollars he wants," said Mom.

"I won't give it to him until he shows me the ball," Sam promised.

As soon as he saw Bettridge next morning, he asked, "Did you bring it?"

"It's in that shopping bag out there in the long grass back of the goal line," Bettridge answered. "See it? Let me see your two dollars."

Sam took the money from his pocket. As he tried to see the brown shopping bag, Bettridge snatched the money and walked off. He paid no attention when Sam shouted, "Hey, wait!"

Sam felt a little sick. Suppose there was no shopping bag.

Or suppose the ball inside it was old and soft as a rotten apple.

6

The General Comes Again

As fast as he could go with a broken arm, Sam ran to find the shopping bag. It was there. He reached in. Out rolled a soccer ball—new and hard, all clean black and white. And it was *his*. It made his heart beat faster just to kick it.

Ricco saw him kicking it along the sideline. "Is that yours, Sam?" he called. "Have you discovered soccer is the game for you?"

Sam laughed with happy excitement. He swung his foot at the ball, sending it nearer to the coach. Ricco said, "You should practice at home, kicking against the side of the house or garage. Don't kick too hard. Then you can meet the ball as it bounces back, and kick it at the wall again. See how many times you can do this without letting the ball get past you. Some of the world's greatest soccer players started that way, when they were younger than you."

Boys gathered around to see the new ball. One of them said, "You always wanted to play baseball, Sam. How come you got this?"

Sam saw Bettridge frown and shake his head. So he kept still about why he got the ball. At the same moment, Red said, "A clean ball like this is easier to see. We ought to have a new one to practice with. How about it, Ricco?"

Sam thought Bettridge would speak up and offer to get a bargain ball for the team. When he didn't, Sam was pleased that *he* was the one Bettridge chose to do the big favor for.

The boys started practice drills. They let Sam join in, with his new ball. "Be careful not to run and hurt your arm," Ricco told him. "Stand near one goal line. When the ball comes near you, boot it to the middle of the field."

When his own ball came near, Sam saw its white spots already had some grass stain. He hated that. Yet he liked being on the field with the boys. He felt like he was on a team.

Ricco blew the whistle to start a game. Pointing to one sideline, he said to Sam, "Stand outside that touchline."

"I thought that was the sideline," Sam said to Red. "What's the touchline?"

"They're the same thing," Red said. "And the line at each end is the goal line. But only the part between the posts is the *goal*. This is the

part we goal keepers guard." He took his place in the space marked off for the goalie in front of the goal posts.

Sam remembered that the players themselves went after balls that rolled just over the sideline. So he stood way back, where he could kick in a ball that went out too far for a panting player to chase after it. He was glad nobody said, "Let's use Sam's ball." He wiped it off on his pants and put it in a safe place. After a while he remembered he was supposed to check on Lori. He went to look for her.

She was watching the crafts class make puppet heads. "They won't let me do it," she said to him. "Let's go home."

"She wouldn't even try to make a puppet head," said Alison. "She wanted to make a long nose on her own face instead."

"Did I get the stuff all off?" Lori held up her face to Sam. Then she noticed the ball and grabbed it from him. "Is it for me?"

"Where did you get that?" Alison asked.

Sam only said, "It's mine. . . . Are you ready to go home?"

Alison wanted to finish her puppet head. "It's going to be a monkey, if the ears stay on," she said. "If they don't, I'll turn it into a princess with yarn hair."

Lori wanted to carry the ball. The first thing she did when they got home was to roll it across the floor. "Look, Mommy! Look! It twinkles!" She clapped her hands. "Wait till Fearless sees it."

Fearless was stretched under the table. He sprang to his feet when he saw the ball coming. He started to hump his back and hiss. The whirling, spotted ball kept coming straight at him. Fearless fled.

"Now we know how to make him behave."

Sam laughed. "We'll roll my soccer ball at him."

"Remember—" Mom held up one finger, "—you are not to play with it until your arm is well."

"You don't throw this kind of ball," Sam said. "You kick it—like this."

He kicked harder than he meant to. The ball sailed into the next room, hit a chair, and slammed it against the wall.

"Oh, dear," Mom groaned.

Sam quickly said, "It didn't break."

"Maybe the chair didn't break," Mom said. "But it knocked a chunk of plaster out of the wall." As she felt the hole, more fell out. The floor below was white with plaster crumbs. "Oh, dear!"

Sam tried to roll the ball out of sight with his foot. She frowned and started to say something.

"Wait!" he stopped her. "Somebody is coming to the front door."

Before they heard the doorbell, Sam was already there. "Oh, General! It's you! Come on in. I'm awfully glad to see you. . . . Hey, Mom! It's the general!"

"Oh—" She tried to smile as the roly-poly man followed Sam into the room. "Oh—hello."

The general gave her a quiet look. "Is something wrong, Mrs. Blake?"

Sam answered for her. "I just knocked a hole in the wall with my new soccer ball." He pointed to the place. "I didn't mean to."

The general took a closer look at it. He turned to Mom with a big smile on his round face. "Don't worry about a little thing like this. I'll fix it right away. I have some stuff on my truck to patch plaster."

"You and your truck must be magic," Mom said. She looked happier now. "You always appear when something needs mending. And your truck always has whatever is needed to do the job."

The general laughed till his eyes squeezed shut. "By jingo, that's what I'm for. But nobody ever called it magic. I'll be back in a jiffy. You spread some newspapers on the floor under that crack."

Sam started to follow. Mom kept him to help spread the newspapers. As they finished, the general came back with a box of white powder, a mixing pan, a putty knife, and rags. After working at the hole for a few minutes, he sat back on his heels. "How does it look to you?" he asked Mom.

"It's a beautiful job," she said.

"It's not the same color as the wall," Lori said. "I can see where the hole was."

"Just wait, little Miss Bright-eyes. I haven't finished yet." He turned to Mom, saying, "I think I have some green paint that matches your wall, Mrs. Blake. We'll let this plaster dry for a few days. Then I'll come back to finish my job."

As he gathered up his stuff, Sam brought the new ball to show him.

"That's a dandy, Sam," he said. "Where did you get it?"

"Sam made two dollars." Mom laughed and told the story. "So he bought this ball."

"For only two dollars?" The general's eyes opened wide and round. "Where did you get a deal like that?"

"From a boy at the playground." Sam hoped he was not breaking his promise to Bettridge.

"Hmm. How come he has soccer balls to sell?" the general asked.

"I was just going to ask Sam the same thing, when that happened." Mom pointed to the patched wall.

Sam said, "I think his father must be in some kind of business that sells them. So he gets them a lot cheaper than you can buy them in the stores."

The general nodded and started to leave. "I must get going in my magic truck." He went out the door, laughing at the thought.

All three stood in the window to wave good-by. They took a good look at those big white letters on the side of the red truck. GENERAL MAINT.

"He didn't say that isn't his name," said Sam. "But I don't suppose it is."

"It's the name of his business, I think," said Mom. "And he wanted it in very large letters, so people would notice it. But he couldn't get the whole word on the side of the truck."

"What word?" Lori wanted to know.

"Maintenance," said Mom.

"That's his business, Lori." Sam explained, "He fixes things."

Mom added, "Houses and buildings get broken windows and leaky roofs and peeling paint—or cracks in the walls. A general maintenance man is called in to do the repair job. Our man has his telephone number right there on his truck where people can see it."

"That's handy for them," Sam said. "I wonder why he doesn't have his real name there too. I'm going to ask him when he comes back to paint the patch in the wall."

"Ask if he minds if we call him General," said Lori.

As it turned out, he didn't mind at all.

"My name is Stanislav Ruzomberok. That's no name to put on my truck." He smiled. "It's even hard for American people to say."

"Aren't you an American?" Sam asked. "You talk just like us."

"Of course, I'm an American." The round little man stood as tall as he could. "I was born in this country. But my parents came from Czechoslovakia. Ruzomberok is a fine old name in that country. So I do not want to change it. But put it on my truck? No!"

Mom explained why Sam had started calling him "General."

"Please forgive us," she finished.

"What's to forgive? You have made me a general. By jingo, I like that. Don't stop it." He smiled at them. "Now let's mix up a little paint to match your green wall."

While he worked, he asked Sam, "Have you been kicking that new soccer ball around?"

"Not in the house!" Mom said.

The general laughed. "My mother used to say that to me about my soccer ball."

"Did kids play soccer in olden times when you were a boy?" Sam asked.

The general laughed so hard he couldn't hold the paint brush steady. "I'm not quite old enough to remember Noah building the Ark. But I'll bet kids played soccer even then. Or a game very much like it," he said. "I learned it first from my Dad. He was a soccer player in the old country."

"Really?" Sam asked. "Do they know about soccer there?"

"Hmf!" the general snorted. "In almost every country but this one, soccer is Number 1. Just play it once. You'll discover it's the most exciting game in the world."

"I like baseball best," said Sam.

The general chuckled. "There are people who like plain vanilla ice cream best—until they taste a chocolate sundae."

7

Sam in Real Trouble

Without another word the general finished painting and cleaned his brush. When Mom brought her pocketbook to pay him, he shook his head. "I never charge for repairing damage done by soccer balls," he chuckled. Then he asked Sam, "Have you ever tried to play soccer? I read in the paper that teams from the playground have started a league. You're old enough to be in it, aren't you?"

Sam quickly said, "I can't play with my arm in a cast."

"No, of course not. But where I grew up, boys started kicking a soccer ball before they even started school."

"I do that." Sam started to hunt his ball. "I'll show you how good I'm getting."

"Not in the house!" That was Mom again. The general laughed.

66

Sam took the ball outdoors. The general followed and watched him kick it. Lori ran to get it. Sam waited for the general to tell him he was "a natural-born soccer player."

The general only said, "Don't run little Lori's legs off. Short kicks are needed in soccer too. Try some. And try kicking backwards. That kick comes in handy in a game."

"How do I do it?" Sam asked.

"Put the ball on the ground just behind you. Like this. Then kick it backwards with your heel."

Sam tried it. "Hey, it's real tricky. I never saw anybody kick that way. I'll pull it on the guys at the playground."

Next morning he started out with his new ball under his arm.

"What are you bringing that for?" Alison asked. "You never want to play anything but baseball."

"This ball is prettier than a baseball," Lori said. "Show her how it twinkles, Sam."

Sam put the ball on the sidewalk. He turned around and kicked it with his heel. He really did like to kick that ball. With Lori to run after it, he kicked it all the way to the playground. Backwards.

He planned to wait where he stood yesterday, away from the sideline. Then when the ball rolled off the field toward him, he would turn his back on it. The boys would think he wouldn't bother to return it to them. But—surprise!—he would send it back with his heel kick.

When he got to the field, most of the boys seemed to be looking at Chuck's new shoes. Somebody said, "Man, those are beamy!" Another boy said, "If I had a pair of those, I'll bet I could play better."

Sam saw Chuck was wearing black shoes with white stripes across them. They had knobs on the bottom. Red asked, "Where did you get the soccer shoes, Chuck?"

Chuck did not answer. Sam remembered seeing shoes like that in a store window. He spoke up, "You can buy them at the sporting goods store."

"We didn't know that," Bill Bettridge said in a nasty way. He pretended to be very surprised. "We thought you buy them at the bakery."

Sam didn't laugh with the others. He wondered why Bettridge made fun of him now, after treating him like a good friend a few days ago.

Ricco said, "It's fine to have soccer shoes. But I think the sneakers most of you are wearing will do just as well. Now, let's help Chuck break in those expensive shoes in a game." He blew his whistle. "Take your positions, men!"

Sam went to his spot. He thought the ball

would never come his way. The players kept it going all over the field. Suddenly someone's kick was blocked. The ball spurted toward the touchline and came rolling straight at Sam. He whirled around and gave it a hard punch with his heel.

Red yelled, "Yowie, look at Sam!"

Just then Ricco called time-out to let the boys catch their breath. He came to the sideline. "Hurry and get out of that cast, Sam," he said with a smile. "We can use a kicker like you."

Practice started again. A moment later somebody over on the baseball diamond hit an extra long one. The ball struck a stone and bounced almost to Sam's feet. He carried it back. For a while he stood looking on, waiting for a batter to get a base hit. Baseball seemed awfully slow to him, after the speed and flash of soccer.

"Sa-a-am!" He heard Lori calling. "Sa-a-am!"

Here she came, carrying something as if it were a queen's crown. "Looky, Sam! I made it in crafts. It's a little bowl for Fearless to drink out of."

"I don't think it's big enough," he said.

"Fearless has a tiny mouth."

"He has long whiskers, too. Cats like room for their whiskers when they drink," Sam said.

"Let's go home and see if this fits him." Lori pulled Sam's sleeve.

"I have to get my ball first. I left it over at the soccer field." Sam started away.

"I'll come with you," she said.

"No. You go wait with Al. I want to ask Red something." Sam felt the red-haired goal keeper was a friend. So now he asked Red the question on his mind.

"Ricco said we—you—play your first game with another team in three weeks. Is that the start of the play-offs? Will summer playgrounds close when the play-off games are over?"

Sam still hoped there would be time for him to play baseball after his cast was off.

"The playgrounds close the week before school starts. But the soccer league is new this year," Red explained. "It isn't going to have play-offs. There will be one game every week. At the end, the team with the most wins will be the champion. Its players will get City Champ patches. So will the eleven boys on its second team."

"Even the second team?" Sam asked.

"Sure. They earn them! There wouldn't be any first teams without second teams to practice with."

Sam nodded. He was glad champ patches were awarded to second teams. This gave him a better chance to win one himself in baseball. If his arm would only heal fast enough!

He asked the doctor about that next time he was called in to have it checked. All Dr. Kraft said was, "It's coming along nicely." He wouldn't give a hint about when he would take off the cast.

The morning after his check-up, Sam turned up at soccer practice.

"You should have been here yesterday," Red said right away. "We played the boys from Croswell playground. Now we've got one game under our belts."

"You mean we—you—won?"

"Four to nothing! You should have seen Bettridge. Nobody can beat us with him in there. He made all our goals."

Sam was sorry he missed the game. He asked, "Will you play another team next week? Where?"

"Here. This is the best soccer field in town. Next week we play Central. That will be a tough one. They won their first game 12 to 4."

Sam noticed that the boys were working hard at practice. They wanted their City Champ patches as much as he did. Bettridge kept telling them, "We'll win. Just feed the ball to me. Keep their men out of my way, and I'll make the goals."

He made all three goals against Central. Red, at goalie, held them to two. When the game ended, Sam ran to crowd around Bettridge. Then he saw Red on the ground in front of his goal.

"Whoof!" Red was grinning and gasping for breath at the same time. "I'm pooped. That sure was a squeaker."

"You're a star goal keeper, Red. We couldn't have done it without you," Ricco praised him. He helped the player to stand up. "Are you all right?"

"Sure. I'm fine. Whoof!" Red let out another gasp. "I just hope we can win the *easy* way next week."

"All we have to do is pass the ball to Bettridge," somebody said.

That was the way they played the next game. They counted on Red to keep the other team from scoring. Bettridge kicked the ball past the enemy's goal keeper seven times in the first half.

Then Ricco took him out of the game. "Let's not trample all over them," he said. "That's not real sport. We'll make it a better game if we put someone else in Bettridge's place. Chuck, you go in at center forward."

Bettridge blew up at that. Ricco said, "Keep your cool, fellow. You will have plenty of chances to make goals in our other games. Let Chuck have his chance now."

As it turned out, Bettridge made the winning goals in the next two games.

"We've been riding high for five weeks, men," Ricco said. "Let's not take a tumble in our last game. As you know, Westgate also has won all its games so far. If we can beat them—"

"We'll be Number 1!" the boys shouted. "Hurray!"

Sam shouted with them. He hoped the baseball team would be champions too. But he felt he belonged more to soccer now. He spent that whole afternoon kicking his soccer ball around the neighborhood with Alison and Lori.

Just before dinner, the doorbell rang. "I'll go," Sam called to his mother. "Maybe it's the general."

It wasn't the general. It was a police officer. He asked, "Does the Blake family live here?"

"Y-y-yes," Sam stammered.

"Is there a boy in the family named Sam?" the officer asked.

Sam was scared. He swallowed hard and squeaked, "Me."

"I would like to talk to your parents. May I come inside?"

Sam unlatched the screen door, then ran to the kitchen.

"Mom!" he whispered. "It's a policeman. I think he's after me. But I didn't do anything. Honest, I didn't. You know I didn't, Mom!"

"He's probably looking for a different Sam Blake," she said. "I'll straighten it out." She put her arm around him and walked with him to the front door. Lori followed with Fearless at her heels.

The officer was standing inside the door. "Are you Mrs. Blake?" he asked. "This boy's mother?"

"Yes." She gave Sam a little squeeze. "And I'm proud of him too."

The officer looked at his note pad. "We have a

report that he has been seen with stolen property."

Mrs. Blake laughed. "I haven't seen my son with any stolen property. You must have the wrong boy."

"No." The officer looked at his notes again. "Everything checks out. Name. Address. Description of the boy."

"I didn't steal anything," Sam said. "Honest, Mom."

She said, "Officer, my son does not lie. If he says he did not steal anything, he didn't."

"Hmmm." The officer looked from one to the other. "Perhaps he *received* stolen property. Maybe he bought it."

"How could he?" she asked. "His small allowance goes at once for bubble gum and popsicles. He never has any other money to spend."

"Except that two dollars," Sam reminded her. "What the lady gave me for the pitcher."

The officer pounced with his next question. "Where did you get the pitcher?"

"He bid on it at an auction," Mom said quickly.

"How could he? You said he never has any money except his small allowance."

"That's right," Sam answered for her. "The two dollars the lady paid me for the pitcher was extra money."

"Let me get this straight, Mrs. Blake." The

officer set his cap on the floor. He took out his
pen, ready to write on his note pad. "You and
your son say he had no money. Yet he got this
pitcher at an auction. Later, he sold it for two
dollars. What I want to know is how he paid for
it in the first place. *If* he did."

"I didn't," Sam said. "A lady—" He stopped to
see what the policeman was writing.

The officer read it aloud. " 'Boy admits he sold a pitcher he did not pay for.' . . . Is that correct, Mrs. Blake?"

At that moment Sam's soccer ball came rolling past him. Lori said later she did it because Fearless had climbed into the policeman's cap. She was afraid this would make the officer mad, and he would take them all to jail. So she tried to scare the cat away with the soccer ball. The instant Fearless saw it coming—*zzzt!*—he shot for the kitchen.

The officer saw the ball too. "Ha! This looks like new. Where did you get it?" he asked Sam.

"I bought it."

"But you and your mother say you get only a small allowance. Soccer balls cost twelve to fifteen dollars." He looked at his notes again. "It says here that a soccer ball is among the stolen articles in this case we are investigating."

"That must be some other soccer ball, officer. My son didn't steal this one. He bought it from a friend."

"What is the friend's name?"

"Bill Bettridge," said Sam.

"Where does he live?"

"I don't know," said Sam.

The officer gave him a sharp look. Then, after another look at his notes, he said, "That name checks out. And a soccer ball is one of the things stolen from the sporting goods store on Main Street."

"I didn't steal it!" Sam cried out.

"Even if you didn't steal it yourself—" the officer wrote on his paid,"—you are in possession of stolen property. You could be arrested right along with the real thief."

8

Will Sam Be Sent to Jail?

"I didn't steal it!" Sam felt tears rolling down his cheeks. "I didn't steal anything!"

"If he didn't—" the officer looked at Mrs. Blake, "—how come he has this soccer ball exactly like the one that was stolen? He admits he didn't buy it from the store."

"We told you. He bought it from that other boy," Mrs. Blake said quietly. "*He* is the one who must have stolen it. That means Sam has done nothing wrong."

The officer shook his head. "No. It means Sam has committed the crime of receiving stolen property. The laws of our state say a person can be sent to jail for this."

Jail. The word seemed to grab Sam by the throat. He was too scared to speak.

"Receiving stolen property sometimes means

jail for up to three months, or a fine of $300. Or both," said the policeman.

Mom cried out, "But Sam had no idea the ball was stolen!"

At that moment a roly-poly shape appeared outside the screen door. "Do you folks need any help?" asked a familiar voice.

"General! Oh, *General!*" Sam was so glad to see his old friend. "Come in, come in!"

The general explained, "I was going by and saw the police car out front. I figured you might be in some kind of trouble, so—"

"He is." The officer turned around to see who had come in.

"Why, hello, Elzy," the general greeted him. Sam thought it was like that day at the hospital. The general knew everybody.

"My wife has been going to call you," the officer said. "She wants you to come and take some squeaks out of the kitchen floor."

"Be glad to." The general brushed the matter aside to ask, "What brings you here, Elzy? I know this boy. He isn't the kind to get into trouble."

"Well, he's in it up to his neck." The officer told the story. "So you see, he'll have to be taken into court. Either he has been receiving stolen property, or else he stole this ball himself."

"He did no such thing," said the general. "I

know how Sam got that ball. He didn't know it was stolen. The older boy offered him a bargain. Sam took it. Any kid would. Especially if he had a natural soccer kick, like Sam."

Officer Elzy scratched his head. "But surely Sam must have known the ball was stolen property. Why did he think a boy would have brand-new balls to sell cheap?"

"We talked about that. Remember?" The general looked at Sam and his mother.

Sam felt better with his friend standing by him. He answered for himself, "I thought his father had a store and got things cut-rate."

"Didn't you ask the other boys?"

"No, sir. He made me promise I wouldn't tell them I got it from him."

"That may be true." Officer Elzy looked at the general. "On the other hand, we have a report that this boy was in on the shoplifting."

"Forget it, Elzy. Could anybody shoplift with one arm in a cast?" The general put his hand on Sam's shoulder. "You won't take this boy into court, will you? If you do that, I want to go with him. I'll prove to the judge that Sam did nothing wrong."

The officer looked at his notes before he closed the book. "I think I have all we need from Sam—and from you, too. We won't have to call him into court."

"Good. Now you get in your cruiser and lead the way to your house. I'll see what I can do for your wife's squeaky floor."

As the officer left, he picked up the ball. "We will keep this at headquarters," he said. "It may be needed for evidence against the shoplifters."

Sam held his breath until the two men were gone. Then his knees would not hold him up any longer. He and Mom both sank down on the sofa.

Lori asked, "What's shoplifting?"

Sam said, "I heard some talk about it on the six o'clock news last night. But I didn't pay much attention. What did they say, Mom?"

"They said there is a lot of shoplifting going on. Some stores have hired detectives to watch. If they see some customers slip something off the counter into a shopping bag or pocket, they follow those people outside and arrest them."

"Arrest them?" Sam asked.

"Yes. Shoplifting is stealing. Same as if they got into somebody's house, and stole. The worst part is that boys and girls are doing it. The police think these young shoplifters don't realize they are committing a crime. The kids think it's fun to steal from stores. Then, if they sell the stuff they have stolen, that's another crime."

"That's what Bettridge did, wasn't it?" Sam asked. "What made the police think I did it? How did they ever get my name?"

"When the police caught him, he must have told them about you. He may have said it was you who did the shoplifting," she said. "Did you ever see any of the other boys at the playground with expensive new sweaters or balls or—"

"Chuck's soccer shoes!" Sam suddenly remembered. "The guys said they were real beamy and where did he get them."

"Did he tell them?"

"I don't think so." Sam tried to remember. Then something else popped into his mind. Bettridge at the auction, slipping comic books under his shirt. *Bettridge was a thief.* It hurt Sam that this was true. He remembered when Bettridge offered him the bargain ball. He had been so proud to have for a friend the best player on the soccer team.

"Will—will they put him in jail?" he asked.

"You heard what the policeman said."

Sam nodded. Mom went on, "Still, he is young. He would be sent to reform school instead. Or the judge may let him off easy because this is surely the first time he was caught stealing. I hope you will stay away from him after this. A boy who gets you in trouble with the police is certainly not a friend."

"I know," Sam said slowly. "But the soccer team will lose their last game if they don't have Bettridge. They can't win the championship without him. They wouldn't get their champ patches, either. I'm glad he won't have to stay in jail."

"I'm glad the policeman didn't take Fearless to jail," said Lori. "Or you either, Sam."

"I'm glad the general came when he did," said Mom. "I hope he comes again soon, so we can thank him."

The general came that very evening. He brought Sam a soccer ball. "I sometimes referee soccer games at the 'Y' camp. So I keep a book of rules on my truck, and I always have a ball or two at home. This one isn't as good-looking as the one you lost to the police. But it will do for you to practice with. The important thing," he said, "is to get the feeling for soccer in your feet."

Sam didn't want to think about soccer. It had made enough trouble for him. "I won't need the ball," he said.

"Aren't you going to practice anymore?" The general looked surprised. "Don't you still· want to win that City Champion patch?"

"I'll win one in baseball."

"Do you really believe you can?" the general asked. "Why don't you switch to soccer and be sure of it. Like I always say—there's more than one way to skin a cat."

"Not Fearless!" Lori shouted. "I won't let you!"

The general laughed. "I didn't mean a real cat, girlie. Sam knows what I mean." As he left, he said again, "Remember, Samson—there's more than one way to sk—"

"Don't say it in front of Fearless!" Lori grabbed her cat and held her hands over its ears.

Sam thought he didn't want to see Bettridge ever again. He didn't even want to go back to the playground. He told Alison why, when she stopped by next morning.

"Oh, pidaddle! You don't have to go near the soccer players," she said. "Come along with Lori and me."

"You can do crafts with us," Lori said. "I'm going to work some more on my bowl for Fearless. It's too little for him."

"My puppet's face doesn't look like a princess," Alison said. "I'm going to braid its hair and turn it into an Indian. Why don't you come make a puppet too, Sam?"

"With this?" He held up his arm in its cast.

He ended by going to watch baseball practice. He just stood there, with nothing to do. He kept looking over at the soccer field. He didn't see Bettridge. He went nearer to make sure. He waited behind Red's goal. When the players were all at the other end of the field, he asked Red, "Where's Bettridge?"

"Why?" Red gave him a long look, then said, "I don't want to talk about it. Ask Ricco."

"What will happen to the team?" Sam couldn't help asking. "Red, do you think they will put him in jail?"

"Ask Ricco." Red got ready to kick the ball away as it came near his territory.

Sam noticed that Chuck was playing in Bettridge's place at center forward. Chuck was not playing well. The other boys, too, seemed to have lost their speed. And their kicking was bad. They kept Sam busy returning the ball from far out of bounds. Finally, Ricco blew his whistle. He gathered the boys around him.

"Come over here with us," he called to Sam. "The police told me they talked to you too."

Sam wondered if the boys knew about his soccer ball. How many of them had bought something from Bettridge without knowing he had stolen it?

"Some of you just missed being in serious trouble," Ricco told them. "Bettridge lied about you to the police, trying to save himself. Besides that—well, you know what he did. Would you say a boy like that is a good teammate?"

After a long wait, one spoke up, "He's our best player."

"Yes." Ricco nodded. "But do you trust him to be honest with you?"

Chuck said, "Maybe he won't every do anything like that again."

"I hope he won't," Ricco said. "And when he proves it, we'll welcome him back. But until then, this team is better off without him."

"Westgate will cream us. We'll never win the championship!" The boys groaned.

"If he isn't sent to reform school, why can't he still be on the team?" someone asked.

"He committed a crime," Ricco said. "Anyone who steals is a thief."

"Taking things from stores is just ripping off. It doesn't hurt anybody," Chuck said.

"No matter what you call it, stealing is stealing. And it's wrong." Ricco gave Chuck a sharp look. "Remember, every storekeeper must raise the price of his goods to make up for what has been stolen from him. Shoplifters, like Bettridge, make *you* pay a little more for everything you buy. That's not right either, is it?"

Sam didn't know what to think. He knew he didn't want to be friends with Bettridge. Yet what would the team do without its best player?

"You're better off without him," Ricco said again. "It will surprise you to see what good players you can be. You have been letting Bettridge make the goals, because he always hogged the ball."

"That's true!" Red said. "Now everybody can make goals. Except me."

Ricco smiled at that. "But even with everybody trying hard, we simply can't make enough goals to beat Westgate. Not now. Our only chance now is: *Keep them from scoring.* Fight every second to keep the ball away from them. Stay glued to the man you're guarding. Slide into him sideways and kick the ball away from him. Race after it and pass it to a teammate. Never, *never* stop trying to keep the ball away from our goal line. Don't leave the job to Red alone."

He looked from boy to boy. He nodded as if pleased. "You can do it," he said. "Remember, the word for Westgate is: *Don't let them score.*"

Sam could tell the boys were all fired up to hold Westgate. He wanted to be in the battle too. He wished he would hear them say they needed him at that game, at least to chase balls.

All he heard was, "Sa-a-am! Come look at my little bowl. Do you think it's big enough now?"

9

Wowie for Soccer!

"You're coming to the game, aren't you?" Sam asked Alison on their way to the playground. "Franklin plays Westgate. In soccer. I have to be there to run after the ball when it goes out of bounds."

"Can Fearless and I see the game too?" Lori asked.

"What do you have him along for?" Alison asked.

"I made him a drinking bowl three times, and it was always too little," Lori explained. "This time I am going to try it on him while I make it."

"Well, if you're going to watch Sam's game with me, hold on to Fearless," Alison said. She asked Sam, "How long will it last?"

"Ricco says National Junior Cup games have two halves, thirty minutes each. But at our playground, each half is twenty minutes. And there's ten minutes time-out between. So—" he counted on his fingers,"—so the game will last about an hour. I think. But it won't start for a while."

The girls said they would go to crafts class first. When they heard Ricco's whistle, they would come to the soccer game. Sam went straight to the soccer field. He even forgot to look up as he passed the baseball boys. He was just in time to hear Ricco's talk to the team.

"We still have a chance for the championship. Don't give up! We have won all our games so far. Westgate lost a game. If we hold them to a 0-to-0 tie, they will still be one game behind us. So, *keep the ball away from them.* Don't worry about making goals. Just keep Westgate from making one. Fight every minute to keep the ball among yourselves."

Cars were pulling up to the curb in front of the school building. The Westgate players had arrived. Ricco sent Sam to show them the way back to the soccer field.

He saw a familiar truck coming by. "Hi, General!" he shouted, waving his good arm. "We're having a soccer game!"

The truck stopped. The general stuck out his head. "Samson! I heard about the game! Who's your team playing?"

"Westgate. For the city championship!"

"I'll be right there!" the general shouted. His truck zoomed into a parking place.

Sam noticed some kids from the Westgate playground had come with their team. He followed the last of them to the soccer field. He was glad to see Franklin boys and girls leaving their games and crafts classes to come along. The home team would have rooters too. He saw Alison and Lori with them. Far behind them, the general was coming.

Sam forgot them all when the game started. It went so fast he didn't even remember to watch for balls going out of bounds. It was a good thing each team had its second-string players to do that.

He was busy cheering every time a Franklin player kicked the ball away from a Westgate foot. He let out a "YOW-EE-EE!" every time Red stopped the ball from crossing his goal. By the end of the first half, neither team had scored. Sam crossed his fingers and wished Westgate would not make a goal the last half. He saw Al and told her to do the same. He said to Lori, "You hold onto Fearless. Don't try to cross your fingers."

"Oikey-doikey," she said. "I'll just yell. I'll stay with you so I know when to."

The second half was about to start. The teams

would change goals. Sam wanted to watch from behind Red's goal, so he went to the other end of the field. He was too excited to stop Lori from following.

It was Westgate's turn to make the starting kick. The referee put the ball on the mark in the center of the field. He stepped back and blew his whistle. Westgate's center forward gave the ball a smack toward Franklin's side. Chuck ducked in and kicked it back to Westgate's end of the field. Sam thought Franklin was going to score. Then a Westgate wing cut across, and half a dozen Franklin players rushed to keep the ball away from him. Westgate got it again. They were coming down the field with it. Sam held his breath. Red flung himself on the ground and stretched out in front of his goal to make the save. Sam cheered so hard that Fearless reared out of Lori's arms, sniffed, and shook his whiskers.

The teams were back in the middle of the field now, Westgate trying to move the ball toward Red's goal, Franklin kicking it away. The score was still 0-to-0.

"Hold 'em, Franklin! Hold 'em!" Alison was leading cheers. "Come on, everybody! Let the boys hear it! . . . *Hold 'em, Franklin! Hold 'em!* HOLD 'EM!"

Westgate took the ball again. The battle was fierce around Red's goal. He was scrambling

from one side to the other, up on his knees and down on his stomach, to stop the ball.

"Don't yell so loud!" Lori shouted at Sam. "You're making Fearless nervous. He's acting funny."

Zzzt! Fearless leaped from her arms and shot onto the field. She screamed, "They'll step on him! Get him, Sam! They'll squash him!"

Sam didn't stop to think. He made a dash for the cat. He stumbled and reached out to grab it. At that moment a Westgate forward kicked the ball. It was headed for Franklin's goal. It hit Sam instead. A Franklin player kicked it away. The referee blew his whistle to stop the game. Sam hurried off the field with Fearless.

There were loud cries from the Westgate bunch. They gathered with their players around Franklin's goal. They claimed Sam had cheated them out of a goal. They said the ball was almost to the line, and Franklin's goal keeper could not have got to that side in time to stop it. They said the score was really Westgate 1: Franklin 0. They said the referee was wrong. He said no goal had been made. Therefore Westgate had not scored.

Everybody was getting mad. Sam scolded Lori, "Look what you did! Why did you ever let go of Fearless?"

She started to cry. "I couldn't hold on to him. He wanted to get out there. . . . I don't know what made him do it," she said between sobs.

"Calm down, folks! Hold your fire!" Here came the general onto the field. "Hello, Herman," he greeted the referee. "I went to my truck to get my copy of the official soccer rules. I always keep it handy. You know, I sometimes referee games myself. Now, let's see what it says. . . . Here's what we want. Law 10, part 2: *'A goal cannot be allowed if the ball has been prevented by some outside agent from passing over the goal line.'*

"That's what happened here, isn't it?" The general pointed to Sam. "That boy was an outside agent. He wasn't after the ball. He was trying to save the cat. According to the rules, Westgate did not score a goal. And you, Herman—" he read from his book, "—are *'to start up the game by dropping the ball at the place where the ball came into contact with the outside agent.'*"

"That's right," said the referee. He shouted, "Everybody off the field, so we can finish the game. Everybody but the players—OFF THE FIELD!"

He and the general called Sam to show them the place where he had stopped the ball.

Sam looked around, stooped, and reached out. "About here, I think," he said. "Or maybe here."

The mashed-down weeds under his hand had a smell he remembered. It was that old patch of catnip. No wonder Fearless had gone for it! He laughed to himself.

"This is the place. I'm sure of it," he said to the referee.

The referee dropped the ball there to start the game again. Red crouched at that corner of his goal to protect it. Players fought for the ball. Westgate tried to slam it across the goal line. The ball hit the post and bounced back. A Franklin man gave it a quick sideways kick into the open.

Chuck ran to block Westgate away from it. Back and forth Franklin kicked and dribbled, always keeping the ball from the other team.

Everybody was yelling. Sam was pounding the general with his good hand. The general was so excited he was putting his soccer rules in Sam's pocket instead of his own. He kept asking, "How much time is left?"

At last the referee signaled that time was up. The game ended in a 0-to-0 tie. Franklin was still at the top of the league in games won.

"We're Number 1! We're the champions!" Alison led the cheers as the Franklin players went off the field in glory.

Sam walked off with his old friend. The general gave him a sly poke in the ribs and asked, "What do you think of soccer now?"

"Wow!" was all Sam could say. He was hoarse from yelling and dizzy with excitement. "Oh, *wowie!*"

The general laughed. "Samson, I think you have finally discovered soccer. I'll come around next summer to see you play on the team."

"Do you think they'll want me on it?"

"Sure. You brought them good luck in today's game. After this, they'll want you in all their games."

"Will they want the cat too?" Sam laughed.

"Even without you and the cat, Westgate might not have made that goal. They missed it when they tried again from the same spot, didn't they?"

The general felt in his pockets for his rules book, then saw where he had put it. He chuckled as he reached for it. Starting toward his truck, he added, "Franklin won on a lucky break today. This often happens when two teams are evenly matched. Like I always say—there's more than one way to skin a cat."

The general was right about Ricco and the boys wanting Sam on the team. As the coach explained to him, "Each team in the playground can have twenty-two players, as you know. We lost one, so we'll take you on in his place."

For the first time Sam did not say, "I'd rather play baseball."

He said, "But I can't play like—like *him*."

"I think you will, someday. The thing for you to do now is let this heal." Ricco patted the cast on Sam's arm. "And be sure to come to the playground on the last day. You will want to be with the boys when they get their championship awards."

Sam told Alison about this. She said, "I want to be there too. Our teacher said my Indian girl puppet is very good. I'm going to make her a leather skirt from Mom's old pocketbook. Then she will look more like an Indian. Maybe she'll win a champion patch for me in crafts."

"Do you think the bowl I made for Fearless will win?" Lori asked.

"No," said Sam. "I think it's lopsided."

"I'll come anyway," Lori said. "You can swing me."

On the last morning of summer playground, Alison hurried to the crafts table where the puppets were on display.

Lori made a beeline for a swing and waited for Sam to push her. "Next summer you can push me higher," she said. "You won't have a broken arm."

"Next summer you can push yourself," said he.

Alison came running toward them, waving something. "I won a patch! For my puppet!" she called out as she rushed by. "I'm going home and get Mom to sew it on my sweater right away."

Sam let Lori's swing come to a stop. She said, "Al didn't even show us her patch. I wanted to see it, didn't you?"

What Sam wanted to see was a champion patch of his own, not somebody else's.

He heard, "Hey, Sam!" He saw it was Red

yelling at him. "Come over here with the soccer team."

Sam didn't want to stand by and see more patches given out to other kids. But he went anyway, and stood beside Red. Ricco was saying, "Fellows, we had a fine summer together. I am proud of you. And I'm proud to have coached the winners of the first City Playgrounds Soccer Championship. Now, as I call your names, step forward—"

The boys began to clap. As Ricco spoke each name, a bright red-blue-and-yellow patch flashed from his hand to the boy's. Sam felt sad. The thing he wanted most of all was coming true for these other boys. But not for him.

Then he heard his own name called. What for? He stood there wondering, until the boys started to laugh. Red gave him a friendly push. Only then did Sam see Ricco holding out to him the last of the prize patches.

"For me?" Sam was so excited his voice squeaked. "Are you sure?"

Ricco smiled. "Sure! You're the last man on our second team, and our good luck charm. Next summer, you may be on our first team."

Sam didn't care about next summer. All he wanted was to go back to school in September with that champ patch on his jacket.

When he showed it to Alison, she was surprised. "But you wanted to win a patch for *baseball!*" she said.

"Hah-hah," Sam answered. "There's more than one way to skin a cat."

About the Author

Marion Renick has written many popular books for young readers for which she has received a number of honors, including the Martha Kinney Cooper Ohioana Library Award.

Ms. Renick was born in Ohio and graduated from Wittenberg University. She now lives in Columbus, Ohio, where in addition to her writing she participates in theatre and play productions.

About the Illustrator

David Blossom has illustrated many children's books and magazine articles. He was born in Chicago, Illinois, and now lives with his family in western Connecticut.